DREAMWORKS

Spirit

RIDING FREE

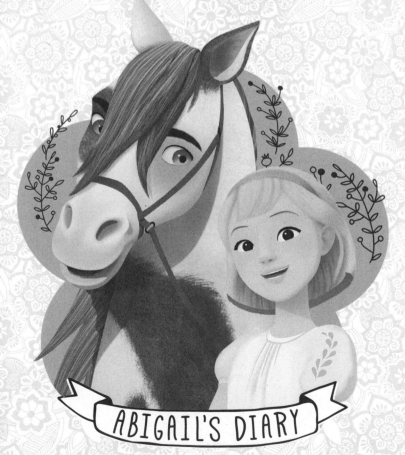

ABIGAIL'S DIARY

Cover design by Ching Chan.

Little, Brown and Company
Hachette Book Group
1290 Avenue of the Americas, New York, NY 10104
Visit us at LBYR.com

First Edition: October 2018

Little, Brown and Company is a division of Hachette Book Group, Inc. The Little, Brown name and logo are trademarks of Hachette Book Group, Inc.

The publisher is not responsible for websites (or their content) that are not owned by the publisher.

Library of Congress Control Number 2018945404

ISBNs: 978-0-316-41356-5 (paper over board), 978-0-316-41357-2 (ebook)

Printed in the United States of America

LSC-C

10 9 8 7 6 5 4 3 2 1

OFFICIAL
MARK OF
SPIRIT

Abigail's Diary

ABIGAIL

STACIA DEUTSCH

Little, Brown and Company

New York Boston

Diary Entry

I've never had a diary before, but thanks to Lucky and Pru, the best PALs ever, I do now. What a nice present! They said I should write down everything about the Frontier Fillies Jamboree because I am so excited.

Wait, hang on a hot minute...maybe they got me the diary so I'd stop talking to <u>them</u> about the Jamboree?

Oh, what am I even thinking? That can't be! That's impossible. Pru and Lucky love hearing me talk about the

Jamboree and all the things we are going to do there.

I mean, who <u>wouldn't</u> want to talk about the Frontier Fillies Jamboree?!

It's going to be the best Frontier Fillies event the frontier has ever seen. At the Fillies Jamboree, everyone can earn badges with their horses!

My brother, Snips, says he's going with us, but he's wrong. He says he doesn't want to be left behind, but that's exactly what's going to happen. Little brothers are not invited, especially not ones like Snips. Only Fillies are invited to the Jamboree.

It's gonna be three whole days of fun with other Frontier Fillies herds from all over. We're going to make

2

friends and eat s'mores and giggle and earn those badges! Lucky is already practicing shooting arrows from Spirit's back for the Boots and Bows mounted archery badge. She's really good at it, too, and never misses the target.

Pru's gone crazy about the talent show badge, which is called the Saddle Showcase. She's been practicing some cool tricks with her horse, Chica Linda. Pru's amazing. I saw her juggling apples while riding Chica Linda over a big jump. She didn't drop even one apple!

I can't wait to earn the Majestic Mare badge. It's about pretty horses. Of course, all horses are pretty to start, so really, it's about prettier horses. Sure, some girls will just groom their horses, clean their tack, and make their horses look nice, but my horse, Boomerang, likes to be way spiffier! I have ribbons, bows, and lace to braid into his mane and tail. I haven't decided what kind of braid would be the best for Boomerang. I can do hunter braids or rosette braids or banded plaits. There are so many choices! This badge was made for Boomerang and me!

The truth is that while I hope to earn all three of the Jamboree badges, there's a bigger pie in the sky: a peach pie with extra whipped cream, and maybe some chocolate baked into the crust. Yeah, the Boots and Bows, the

Saddle Showcase, and the Majestic Mare badges are great, but I really want the Hungerford Heart.

I've been dreaming about it ever since we heard about the Jamboree. I've explained the Heart about a hundred zillion times to Pru and Lucky. I told them about it so many times that they suggested I write it all down in my new diary. Wait, now I'm suspicious again. I mean, how many times is too many times to talk about the one thing I dream about?

The answer is clear: Too many is never enough! I know that my friends love hearing about the Heart. And I'm happy I get to write about it here, too.

So here goes:

The Hungerford Heart is as amazing as it sounds. Ms. Ginger Hungerford—who, by the way, was the one who made us the official Miradero herd—is the founder of the Frontier Fillies. She created the Hungerford Heart award, named in honor of her grandmother, as a gift to the one very special herd that stands out from all the others.

The entire Jamboree votes for the winner of the Hungerford Heart. So that makes it hard to earn. No one can vote for her own herd, so I gotta figure out how to get the others to vote for us.

There's nothing I want more in all the frontier than for the Miradero herd to take home the Hungerford Heart.

The trophy itself is a metal sculpture, forged in the blacksmith shop where Ms. Hungerford's father worked. It's rumored that she forged the metal herself, heating and pounding a long silver bar and then bending it into the shape of a perfectly proportioned heart.

The statue represents the Heart of the Fillies and sits on a cherrywood base that is said to come from the same tree as President George Washington's teeth. Engraved in the base are the four noble virtues of the truest Frontier Filly. Ms. Hungerford's grandmother is said to have been very virtuous and displayed all these best qualities, which is why the award is named for her.

I have the values memorized:

Honor
Compassion
Valor
Honesty

I remember them by HCVH and then thinking of a few of my favorite things: H—Hot dog, C—Cake, V—Vegetables, and H—Hamburger.

See? Not only is the Heart a list of noble virtues, but if I could eat it, it would also be delicious! And that is just one more reason I think the

Miradero herd deserves to take home this year's Hungerford Heart. I mean, I like cooking, so it all makes sense.

I've studied everything I can about the Heart. The descriptive pages in my guidebook are wrinkled and dotted with oily food stains since I like to read and snack at the same time. It's great for focusing and absorbing brain nutrients.

Here's what I've learned: To take home the Hungerford Heart, the Miradero herd must stand out because of our Hot dog, Cake... I mean, Honor, Compassion, Valor, and Honesty.

We've got this. No problem! There's no herd in all the frontier with more HCVH than Pru and Lucky and me! We are the PALs—Pru, Abigail, and Lucky—the worthiest friends.

I have no doubt that after three days at the Frontier Fillies Jamboree, we will earn all three Jamboree badges AND prove to everyone that we deserve the Hungerford Heart.

CHAPTER 1

Did you know the base of the Hungerford Heart is made from the same tree as—"

"George Washington's teeth!" Pru and Lucky exclaimed at the same time. They grinned at each other as they turned their horses down an overgrown path along the dry riverbed.

"Oh." Abigail's eyebrows knitted together. "I guess I already told you about the teeth." Her eyes lit up. "But did I tell you about the silver?"

Pru and Lucky giggled.

"Did you write all about it in your dairy?" Pru asked, turning her head back to Abigail.

"That's why we got it for you," Lucky said, giving Spirit a friendly pat on the neck as the mustang stepped over some large rocks.

"A blank page is the perfect place to share all the good information you know," Pru added. "You know so much about the Frontier Fillies."

"I've got it right here." Reaching down along Boomerang's side, Abigail touched her saddlebag. The diary was tucked inside.

"I already wrote all about the trophy in the diary." She thought for a long moment and said, "In a few hours, we'll be at the Frontier Fillies Jamboree. There will be four other herds there. I bet there are a lot of people who don't know about the engraving at the base of the Heart!"

"And you'll be there to tell them all about it," Lucky said.

"Yes, I will," Abigail said proudly. "I can't wait!"

The rest of the ride was quiet and smooth. The girls turned into a canyon and up a steep mountain trail.

They took two rest breaks on the mountain path to feed and water Chica Linda, Spirit, and Boomerang. Then, at the top of the trail, they made a left at a leafy tree, a right at a cave, another left at a mossy boulder, and finally…the PALs found a spot that looked down on the wide valley where the Frontier Fillies Jamboree was getting underway.

From this view, they could see the dots of colored camping tents. Some tents were up, already billowing in the wind. Others were just being set up. They could see little shadows of Fillies as they moved around the edges of the tents before popping them up for the night.

"Wow." Abigail breathed a long, happy sigh. An open space in the center of the tents caught Abigail's eye. "Let's put our tent there. It's right in the middle, where we can meet all the other Fillies and be friends with everyone."

"I like the way you think," Lucky said, raising her hand to shield her eyes from the sun. "I can't wait to meet the other girls."

Pru was a little more reluctant. "I hope they like us."

"Of course they will!" Abigail assured Pru. "And the more friends we make, the more votes we'll get when we show everyone that we are the most deserving herd."

"Yes, we are!" Lucky cheered.

"Before we get too into meeting people, we better get the horses settled first," Pru reminded the others. "I bet they're hungry and tired." Beyond the tents, there was a temporary riding arena next to a big field. Eight horses were roaming around already, eating the grass in the field. Pru gave Chica Linda a rub on the neck and said, "You're going to make new friends, too, Chica Linda."

Chica Linda whinnied. Boomerang and Spirit picked up the pace, galloping at full speed until they reached the field.

Once Boomerang and Chica Linda had their saddles removed, Spirit led them into the grazing area.

"Have fun, Spirit," Lucky called out.

"We'll see you real soon!" Abigail blew Boomerang a kiss.

"Adiós," Pru said as she gathered up the camping supplies.

The spot they'd picked to put their tent was perfect. Abigail couldn't believe that no one had set up a tent on the wide, flat area.

While laying out supplies, the PALs said a quick "hi" to the girls on their left, who had put up a sign saying:

We're proud to be

the Fillies from Battersea

"We should have made a sign," Pru said. "What rhymes with *Miradero*?" She considered it as they rolled out the tent.

"I got it," Lucky said. "'We're the herd from Miradero! And we're as sharp as an arrow!'" She laughed so hard at her own rhyme that she snorted.

"Now I got one," Pru said, kneeling next to Abigail to hold a tent peg. "Wait…no…it wasn't anything. All I got was the word *sparrow*."

Abigail said, "It doesn't rhyme, but maybe we can write: 'We Hope You'll Vote for Miradero.'" She added, "I could write, 'Please, please, please, please' at the bottom if that's not too much."

"Are you begging for votes?" Suddenly, a tall figure blocked the sun and cast a shadow over where Abigail was about to hammer in Pru's peg.

"If it works," Abigail replied, staying focused

on the peg so she didn't hit Pru's thumb by accident.

"Begging never works," the shadow said. Then it asked, "What are you doing?"

"Setting up our tent," Abigail said, raising the hammer.

"Not here, you aren't."

"Huh?" Abigail lowered the hammer and stood. The girl who faced her wasn't as tall as her long shadow looked. They were, in fact, about the same height. Where Abigail had short blond hair, this girl had long dark hair, braided back with a bandanna tied around her forehead.

"Oh. Hi!" Abigail greeted cheerfully. "We're from Miradero." She quickly introduced Lucky and Pru. "All together, we're the PALs."

"I'm Jimena," the girl told them. She tipped her head toward three girls who also had long hair in braids and wore matching bandannas.

"We are the Golden Valley herd. This is Ana, Olivia, and Riley."

"It's so nice to meet you!" Abigail put out her hand for a welcome shake, but the girls didn't step forward. They stayed behind Jimena.

"You're in our space," Jimena said.

"What?" Abigail didn't understand. She looked around; there was plenty of room for other tents in this one area.

"The herd that has the Hungerford Heart gets the center," Jimena told her. She held out one hand, and Ana set the famous heart-shaped trophy in her palm.

"Oh, oh, oh…" Abigail gasped. She reached out to touch it, but Jimena pulled back the trophy. Abigail shook that off and said, "Did you know the silver came from Ms. Hungerford's—"

"Own town and she forged the metal herself," Jimena finished.

"And the wooden base—"

"Came from the same tree as President Washington's false teeth," Jimena said.

Abigail nodded. "Look, Pru and Lucky!" She pointed to the base. "That's where the Frontier Fillies' values are—"

"Etched." Jimena tapped her finger against the words as she and Abigail recited them together.

"Honor. Compassion. Valor. Honesty."

Pru and Lucky looked at each other, mouths wide open.

"Jimena is the Golden Valley's own Abigail," Pru said.

"I'd never have guessed there was another girl in the world like Abigail," Lucky said. "But here she is."

"You're still in our spot," Jimena said. "You're going to have to move your tent."

"That's ridiculous," Pru told her. "We're almost done here. It's a lot of work to move everything."

Jimena didn't say anything. She simply held the Heart up toward Abigail.

"Right, then," Abigail said, turning to Lucky and Pru. "Pack it up. We're out of here."

"What?" Lucky said. "You're going to let some girl push us out of our prime camp spot simply because she has a bent piece of metal?"

Abigail gasped. "Lucky, it's not bent metal. It's the Hungerford Heart."

Lucky quickly apologized. "Sorry, I know how important that statue is to you. I don't mean to make fun. I just don't think we should have to move." She pointed at an open area near some thick trees. "Golden Valley can have that spot over there. It's more private, anyway."

Abigail looked at the trees and then at

Jimena holding the Heart. She looked back at the trees again. "That's where we'll go," she said, starting to roll up the tent on her own.

Pru and Lucky held back for a moment, then decided they couldn't let Abigail do all the work.

"This is so embarrassing," Pru whispered as they stuffed the tent back into its carry bag.

"I know," replied Lucky. "How do we know they were even telling the truth?"

"Honesty is one of the values that got the Golden Valley their votes." Abigail spoke softly to make sure that Jimena and the others couldn't hear them. "There's no reason to doubt them. If they say that's a rule, it's a rule, even if I didn't know that one. And if the herd that has the Heart gets to pop their tent in the middle of all the others, well, then that's just one more reason that we gotta get it!"

Lucky picked up the tent and they started to walk away. "Yes. That's what we'll do!"

"I'm already working on being more valorous," Pru declared as they reached their new spot near the thick trees. "Whatever that means."

"Thanks," Abigail told her friends. "With you both in my herd, there's no doubt we will get that trophy." They set down the tent in their new spot, ready for a fresh start.

Suddenly, a voice came from the thick trees. "Trophy? Did I hear trophy? I love trophies."

Abigail's eyes went wide. She knew that voice!

Her brother poked his head out from among the leaves of two grand old trees. Next to him, his donkey, Señor Carrots, poked his head out as well.

"Oh no!" Abigail groaned at seeing her brother at the Frontier Fillies Jamboree. "Snips! What are you doing here?"

✿ Diary Entry ✿

Dear Diary,

Snips has to go home!

I am going to admit the truth, but, dear Diary, please don't tell anyone—the thing is, I was honestly a little embarrassed about the whole "tent set up in the wrong place" thing. I know that it'll all work out, and that it was a mistake, and it wasn't a really bad thing, but I'd been hoping for a better start to the Jamboree. Now we have to prove ourselves even more if we want to earn the votes for the Hungerford Heart.

BUT!

Snips will ruin everything if he stays. No, seriously...this is a matter of survival.

Snips says he left a note for Mom and Dad so they won't worry. Snips says he'll stay out of the way. Snips says Señor Carrots can stay hidden in the big trees. Snips has a lot of things to say. But I say...Snips is a pest. Snips will get in the way. And Señor Carrots might be hidden, but he's a noisy donkey and always hungry, too.

UGH!

Why did my parents get me a brother? Couldn't they have gotten another horse instead? It would have

been so much easier, and Boomerang
would love a brother!

<u>UGH!</u>

Okay, Abigail, think....

Here's what I can do:

1) Put Snips on a train back to
Miradero. Nope...that won't
work. There's no train station
near here.

2) Take him home myself. Nope...
that won't work because I'd
have to leave camp to do it,
and by the time I got back, I'd
have missed everything!

3) Send him home by himself.
He followed us here, so he
should know the way. Nope...
what kind of big sister would

I be if I let him go out into the frontier alone? Up that mountain, down the valley, following the riverbed? I'd be the worst sister ever. Which I shouldn't be... even if he's the worst brother ever.

I have a very good idea. I'll send him home in a hot-air balloon. The wind will carry him away from here and straight to Miradero. Sigh. That won't work; I mean, who can predict the wind?

I don't have any more ideas.

I asked Lucky and Pru for some thoughts about what to do with Snips. Pru said we could dress him like a

Filly and pretend he's part of our herd. But that won't work because we don't have an extra uniform. And Snips has never been good at _blending_.

Lucky said Spirit could take him home, but then Lucky would miss the Boots and Bows competition, and I know how much she is looking forward to that one. So that won't work, either.

We're down to my last idea:

4) Let him stay.

I _KNOW!_ That's crazy. It's wacky. It's a very bad idea. But it's the only one I have left that might work.

So...I'm going to tell Snips he can stay at the Jamboree, but he and Señor Carrots both need to stay hidden.

He can't show his face. No one can know he's here. He'll have to stay in our tent all day! Lucky, Pru, and I will bring him food. I'll tell him it'll be an adventure. He can play a game as if he's invisible.

I think Snips will go for it, because if he doesn't... I am going to get a hot-air balloon!

CHAPTER 2

"B ut I don't want to be invisible!" Snips complained when he heard Abigail's idea. "How will I be able to walk if I can't see my feet? I can't eat without my hands. *Invisible?* I want to be *out*-visible!"

"Impossible," Abigail told her brother.

"Out-possible," Snips retorted.

They were all huddled in the Miradero herd's tent, and Pru had zipped up the flap for a private meeting.

Abigail shared a quick look with Pru and Lucky. She hoped they were reading her mind.

"Fine," Abigail told her brother. "If you don't want to stay invisible, you gotta go home. That's the deal." Abigail pointed in the direction of Miradero.

"I will not disappear," Snips protested. "You can't make me."

"Well, then, see ya, Snips. Travel safe." This was a risky move, Abigail knew that, but she had to try. If he stayed, it had to be on her terms—not his. "Bye-bye, Snipsy. Don't let the tent flap hit you on the way out."

Snips didn't move. "Don't rush me, lady. I'm thinking about what to do." He seemed genuinely confused. "Ya see, I've got whatcha call 'a problem.' Mary Pat and Bianca are waiting for me at home. They heard you were away, so they wanted to keep me company the whole time." Snips shivered as if repulsed by the very thought. "That's why I snuck out the window and followed you."

"That's a good reason to stay here," Pru said. She looked hard at Snips. "All you gotta do is stay hidden and you don't have to go back." She smiled. "Or you can leave now. I'm sure the twins will still be waiting on the front porch when you get home. The weekend has barely begun...."

Snips wrinkled his nose and thought a moment. Then he said, "Okay. I'll take the deal. But not because you told me to. I'm staying here because the Miradero herd needs me." He pointed to Lucky, Pru, and Abigail, one by one, then said, "I heard there's a big, shiny trophy. I'm going to help you win it."

"No thanks." That wasn't what Abigail wanted. "We don't need help," she told Snips. "The deal is if you stay at the Jamboree, you have to stay hidden."

"I can hide and help, too," Snips said. "I've got a lot of talents. More talents than fingers to count them on." He waved his hands at her.

Lucky looked to Abigail. "I've got this. Let me explain." She smiled. "Snips, this isn't the winning kind of trophy. It's the Hungerford Heart, and you earn it—well, you don't really earn it, you kind of just act really, really good and then if you are the best at being really good, the herds can vote to give it to you for one year."

Snips looked confused, but Abigail grinned. "Exactly!" She gave Lucky a high five.

Pru turned to Snips. "So, the deal is, if you stay, you stay hidden. No helping, no noise, no…nothing." She glanced out the tent flap. "If you don't like it, you'd better leave before it gets dark. I bet Mary Pat and Bianca have big plans."

Snips gave in. "Oh brother. Fine. I'll do it your way." He spit in his hand and held it out for a shake. "I'll be indivisible."

"Invisible," Abigail corrected, spitting into her own palm.

"Sure," Snips agreed. He pressed his palm against Abigail's, then repeated the spit shake with Lucky and Pru.

"Well, then," Abigail said, wiping her wet hand on her pants. "We're going to lunch. Snips, you stay in the tent, and we'll bring you back a sandwich."

"Don't forget an apple for Señor Carrots," Snips reminded them. He flopped down on Abigail's sleeping bag, put his feet on her pillow, and called out after the PALs, "Yes sirree, I'll be so invisible, no Fillies are gonna know I'm here...."

Lunch was served from a chuck wagon near where the Boots and Bows archery course was set up. Abigail could see Ms. Hungerford standing with a couple of counselors near four large targets. They'd get a chance to earn their first badge that very afternoon.

"I can't wait!" Abigail looked out at the targets. They were large circles set on wheeled carts that could be moved. Ms. Hungerford was studying a clipboard, deciding where the targets would be placed.

"I hope she decides to have them in a big circle," Lucky said. "Then the horses can gallop around the circle, stopping at each target so we can hit it with an arrow." She grinned. "Of course, Spirit and I aren't going to stop." That's what they'd been practicing.

Pru took a lunch tray and led the others toward the fire pit, where the herds were sitting to eat. "I'll admit it: I'm a little worried about getting the Boots and Bows badge," she said. "Shooting arrows while riding isn't really my strongest skill."

"You need to hit only three out of four targets to get the badge," Abigail told her. "You can do that!" She added, "No pressure, but I think we all need to earn all the badges so we can be in the running for the Hungerford Heart. It says in the handbook that 'earning badges is one way to show you're a virtuous herd.'"

"We are a virtuous herd!" Lucky said. She touched Pru's arm. "You can do it. I know you can."

Logs were placed in a circle around the fire pit where the girls could sit for lunch. Pru picked the end of a long log and sat down. "I'll admit that I have been so worried that I started practicing a little at home...."

"What?!" Abigail and Lucky exclaimed at the same time.

"I'm not saying I'm as good as Lucky, but I'm not as bad as Abigail, either," Pru teased, laughing a little.

"Hey!" Abigail began to protest, but then she gave in. "All right. I stink at riding and shooting arrows at the same time. It's too many things: I don't understand how to stay steady on Boomerang while pulling back the bow, placing the arrow, *and* aiming." She shrugged. "It's a lot to do all at one time." She raised her chin and announced, "But I'm focused and ready. If earning the Heart means I gotta hit those targets, I am going to do it!"

"Be happy with the badges, because you don't have a shot at earning the Hungerford Heart," said Ana, from the Golden Valley herd. She balanced her tray on her knees and sat by Pru. Olivia and Riley joined Lucky and Abigail on the next log over.

Abigail said, "It says in the handbook, page thirty-one, second paragraph, that the Heart is given to the herd that embodies the four virtues. That could be anyone."

"True," Ana said. Her long blond hair was a darker color than Abigail's, and she was still wearing the bandanna around her forehead. "But ever since there was a Hungerford Heart, the Golden Valley herd has taken it home—"

Riley interrupted. "In fact, before us, Jimena's mom was in the Golden Valley herd and they held the Heart for years, until Jimena was old enough to come to the Jamboree, and then our herd got it."

"We always get the most votes," Ana said.

Lucky shrugged. "Maybe your luck is changing."

Jimena arrived with her tray. She sat down between Abigail and Ana.

"I hear you're going to try to get the Hungerford Heart," Jimena said to Abigail. There was a challenge in her voice that Pru responded to.

"We're noble and honest and the other stuff," Pru chimed in. "We'll show you."

"Noble isn't part of it," Jimena said, finishing her sandwich. "But you can try."

"We will!" Pru said so firmly that Lucky had to put a hand on her leg to keep her from jumping up off the log. "The Heart will be ours this year; you'll see. We're gonna be so virtuous that there's no doubt in anyone's mind that they should vote for us. We'll win that trophy!" She turned to Abigail. "I need you to teach me all about the Heart. I need to wrap my head around what we need to do."

"I'm in, too," Lucky told Abigail. "Teach me, too!"

Abigail wasn't sure what they could do exactly to prove they were virtuous and get the votes they needed, but she'd do her best. "We'll start tonight," Abigail told her friends.

"Challenge on," Jimena said. "May the best herd take home the Heart." She shared a laugh with Ana, Olivia, and Riley.

With that, the girls settled back to focus on lunch. Jimena looked down at her tray. "Hey," she said, "where's my apple?"

A girl from across the fire pit realized half her sandwich was gone.

Another girl was missing her chips.

The entire Silver Springs herd had chosen carrots, and all their carrots were missing.

Almost everyone was missing food…but no one had seen who'd taken it.

"It's like a ghost or someone invisible!" Olivia exclaimed.

"*Invisible?* That gives me a bad feeling," Lucky whispered to Pru and Abigail. "Someone invisible got hungry…."

"And his carrot-loving donkey, too," Pru whispered back.

The three PALs stood up and slowly moved away from the fire pit to sneak back to the tent. They were going to try again to explain to Snips what *invisible* meant. But before they could get away, an apple core hit Jimena in the back of the head.

Jimena picked it up. "My apple."

Abigail was pretty sure she knew who'd thrown the apple. She looked around, and, sure enough, there was Snips, peeking out between two trees, grinning and waving at her. "Drat," he said, loud enough for her to hear. "I missed."

From that, Abigail knew the apple had been aimed at *her* head, and she knew he'd try again. Determination ran in the family blood, like honey through a beehive. When she looked again, Snips had disappeared.

A second later, a sandwich crust flew past Abigail's ear and hit a girl from Battersea in

40

the eye. The girl didn't get mad. She laughed and threw her own sandwich crust at the girl who she thought threw it. That girl threw an apple core, which hit another girl, and after that...the food fight picked up speed.

"Oh no!" Abigail exclaimed. She ducked as half a banana nearly hit her in the face. "I didn't even know there were bananas at lunch! I like bananas much better than carrots."

"We've got to do something," Lucky said. "How do we stop this?"

Pru tipped up her tray to use as a shield. "We gotta find Snips!"

The girls ran fast and were almost at their tent when Ms. Hungerford stepped into their path. Abigail skidded to a stop so suddenly that Pru and Lucky bumped into her back.

"Eep," Abigail said as she looked up into the stern, unhappy face of Ms. Hungerford.

"U-uh," she stuttered, unsure of what to say. "Hi."

"Going somewhere, girls?" Ms. Hungerford asked, putting her hands on her hips. "A herd who truly wanted to earn the Hungerford Heart would tell their friends to stop throwing food around."

"Right," Abigail said, glancing over at their tent. Snips waved at her from the trees. "Okay." She turned back toward the food fight. "We'll stop this."

"But we didn't start it," Pru argued.

"Sni—" Lucky began, when Abigail grabbed her hand.

"We'll take care of it, Ms. Hungerford," Abigail said, and in a blink she was leading her friends back into the war zone.

The problem with stopping the food fight was that everyone was having a great time.

Jimena had a slice of turkey in her hair and was laughing. Ana was tossing an apple core back and forth with a girl named Sophie from Copper Point.

"Stop!" Pru called out. No one listened.

"We gotta clean up!" Lucky shouted. No one listened.

Lucky started catching half-eaten carrots as they flew past her, while Pru began swiping half-eaten scraps that were skidding across the ground.

Abigail shook her head. "We'll never earn the Hungerford Heart this way."

"Enough!" Ms. Hungerford whistled loud and clear. The girls all fell silent. "I see that I have to take matters into my own hands. Lunch is over. Food fights are not in the handbook, and I expect my Fillies to behave better." Her glare fell on Jimena and the

Golden Valley herd. "You are the keepers of the Hungerford Heart. What do you have to say for yourselves?"

Jimena looked at the ground and stayed silent.

Abigail was horrified. She could feel the trophy slipping from her dreams. Boldly stepping forward, head high, she said, "I'm so sorry, Ms. Hungerford. Don't worry. The Miradero herd will clean everything up."

"What?! But we didn't do—" Pru started, but Lucky held her back.

"Of course we will," Lucky said. Then to Pru she whispered, "We're helping Abigail."

"Right." Pru nodded. She stepped next to Abigail.

As the other herds hurried away to change clothes and get ready to earn the Boots and Bows badge, Abigail, Pru, and Lucky cleaned up bits of food from the ground.

"Why'd you volunteer to clean up?" Pru asked Abigail, while stuffing apple cores in a metal bucket.

Abigail paused, and then she said, "Snips started the food fight. We can't tell anyone about Snips, so that means it's as if we started the food fight."

"Does that make sense?" Pru asked Lucky.

"Maybe?" Lucky shrugged.

"Food fights are fun when you get to play along," Pru said with a sigh. "Cleaning up isn't."

"We can make this more fun," suggested Abigail. "Let's play a game. Hold up your bucket." Pru did so and Abigail tossed in apple cores. Pru moved around to make it more challenging. Lucky got into the fun, and they took turns holding the bucket and tossing in food. In no time, it was all cleaned up.

"We have to hurry," Lucky said, looking

over at the field where girls were already gathering with their horses.

"Boomerang and Chica Linda both need saddles," Pru noted.

"You two go on ahead of me. I want to yell at Snips," Abigail said. "I'm a good yeller. I'll do it fast." She rushed to the tent, but when Abigail opened the tent flap to have a heart-to-heart about the Heart with her troublemaker brother, she was surprised to find the tent was empty.

Snips was gone.

✿ Diary Entry ✿

Dear Diary,

Jimena's herd is going first for the Boots and Bows badge, so even though we hurried over, now we wait. I have time to write a few thoughts.

I'm worried that Ms. Hungerford is mad. That's gotta change. I don't know how to make things better, but I think if we stick like maple syrup to living by the virtues in the handbook, we'll not only survive this weekend but still have a chance at the Hungerford Heart.

We've looked all over the campsite but can't find Snips. I don't know where he is, but just wait till we get back to the tent tonight! He's gonna wish he was still hiding! Yeah...

Speaking of tonight, I am going to teach Pru and Lucky more about the values, so I thought I should prepare a little. Just like Mrs. Prescott, I'm gonna act like a teacher. A Frontier Fillies teacher.

First I'll remind them that it's easy to remember HCVH. I think Pru should remember it by the sentence Hero Chooses Velvet Halter. Lucky could remember the letters by using something about Spirit's wild herd— maybe Herd Champion Visits Horses.

48

I think I'll stick with Hot dog,
Cake, Vegetables, and Hamburger.

So, starting with Hot dog—I mean,
Honor. Honor means having the guts
to do what's right, even if others aren't
doing what's right. It's about showing
consideration to everyone. A person
with honor stands up against trickery
and does not brag about their successes.
Honor is the opposite of what Snips
is doing. He's not standing up against
trickery—he's causing trickery! You
know who does have honor? Horses.
All horses. Everywhere. They do what
is right, not because they have to or
because they get to brag about it at the
herd meet-up later, but horses are just
good and noble all the time. That is

what honor is all about. I'll tell Pru and Lucky: Be like a horse and not like Snips. They'll totally get what I mean.

C is for Compassion. This one is easy. Compassion is showing love for others: people, animals, plants...anything. Compassion is treating someone nicely, the same way you'd want to be treated. Pru's mom is best. Mrs. Granger cares about everyone: horses and people, too. You know who else has a lot of compassion? Miss Flores, that's who. Mrs. Prescott, I mean. She loves everyone. Of course, she loves Mr. Prescott the most, but she still has room in her heart for all of us.

<u>Valor</u> is the courage to stand up for what's right, even if it's risky. Valor can be little things, like eating something that looks gross, but true valor is courage times a hundred. It's like that feeling when you are riding your horse and you see a big jump coming up, and your heart is racing and you think, <u>I should just stop this horse and go home</u>, but then you don't stop the horse and you face a huge fear, and the horse jumps and lands safely on the other side and you had valor. It doesn't have to be a horse, but jumping is an important part of valor. Get it?

<u>Honesty</u> means having respect for the truth. An honest person tells no

lies. This might be the most important value for a Frontier Filly. A Filly is supposed to be truthful and sincere. You should always be able to trust a Filly. She's honest in her words and her heart and her mind. Her words speak only truth. I have a bad feeling that I might be bending this value a lot by telling Snips to be invisible, but maybe since Pru and Lucky know the truth, that balances the fact that no one else does? Honesty is important and sometimes really hard. I mean...

Whoa, hang on—I gotta go. I hear Lucky and Pru calling my name. Something weird is happening at Boots and Bows.

CHAPTER 3

L ucky and Pru came rushing up to Abigail.
"You aren't going to believe what's
going on!" Lucky told her, grabbing Abigail's
arm and dragging her toward the starting
block. It was actually a pile of hay bales with
a sign on it that said, BEGIN HERE.

The Golden Valley herd was up. As the
Hungerford Heart holders, they would get
to go first at every event and get the chance
to earn their badges before any of the other
herds. Pru thought that wasn't fair. She
thought there should be a competition to
see who went first, like a race, but Abigail
explained that on this, the handbook was
clear—the herd with the Heart went first.

"What's going on?" Abigail asked Pru.

"We have a problem," Pru said. "Riley, Olivia, and Jimena already had their turns. They didn't hit any targets at all."

"None at all?"

"None," Lucky confirmed.

"That seems impossible," Abigail said, looking to see that Ana of Golden Valley was sitting on her horse. She was yellow with white patches on her rear. "Cupcake," Abigail remarked. At Pru's questioning look, she explained, "I've been getting to know all the horses."

"She's an Appaloosa with a long nose," Pru noted. "I like her Palomino coloring."

"It's starting." Lucky got very serious. "Cupcake and Ana are ready for action." She pointed to where Ms. Hungerford stood in the distance, ready to blow the starting horn and check off on her clipboard when the arrows hit the targets.

They moved closer to watch.

"I hope Ana does better than Riley, Olivia, and Jimena," Sophie was telling a girl from the Lakeside herd.

"I can't believe they missed every target," the girl replied. "They didn't even have to get a bull's-eye, but they hit nothing at all. I think they'll have to try to earn the badge again next year."

Abigail knew you didn't have to earn all the badges to win the Heart, but, still, it sure helped. She leaned in to Lucky and Pru. "I thought you were kidding. Jimena, Olivia, and Riley really didn't hit the targets?"

Lucky shook her head. "Not even one arrow."

"Keep your eyes on the targets," Pru told Abigail. "Don't blink."

Abigail stared straight out, which was hard in the bright sunlight. Her eyes started to water as Ms. Hungerford blew the horn. The sound of the starting toot echoed through the valley, and an instant later, Ana and Cupcake were off and running.

"She's a good rider," Pru told Lucky and Abigail. "I'd love to compete against her in the riding ring."

"It's not a competition!" Abigail and Lucky said at the same time.

"I know!" Pru chuckled.

Abigail focused on Ana's next move. She slowed as she reached the first target. Not everyone could shoot an arrow and ride like Lucky on Spirit. Most of the girls had to stop at the targets. It didn't make a difference for the badge. Land an arrow in three out of four targets and the little circle patch with an arrow on it was yours.

Ana approached the target. She reined Cupcake to a halt and raised the bow that had been tied to the saddle. The arrows were in a case that hung across Ana's back. Like a warrior, Ana reached behind her and grabbed an arrow.

"She looks like a pro," Abigail said. "I'm guessing she'll get a bull's-eye."

"Probably not," Pru said, and Lucky agreed.

"Huh?" Abigail asked. Lucky and Pru pointed.

"Eyes on the target," Pru reminded her. "Just watch what happens."

Ana steadied her bow. Pulled back the arrow and aimed.

What happened next was so fast that Abigail could barely believe her eyes. The arrow soared through the air, straight and true—headed directly into that small red bull's-eye.

It got closer and closer and then, just before the arrow hit the target, the target rolled away.

It was subtle, and maybe the other Fillies didn't see it, but Abigail had been staring hard at the target.

"It moved!" she said to Lucky and Pru as the arrow flew right past the target and landed in the dirt.

"We know," Lucky said. "I was watching Jimena shoot, since she went first. She doesn't need to stop on her horse—" She paused for Pru to fill in the name.

"I don't know the name." Pru shrugged. "But I know she's an Appaloosa."

"Duchess," Abigail put in. "She calls her horse Duchess."

"Right," Lucky said. "Duchess rode past the target, and Jimena took what I thought was a perfect shot, but she missed. And she missed the next three targets, too!"

As Lucky explained, Abigail watched Ana and Cupcake gallop to the next target, stop, shoot, and miss. The third was the same, and by the fourth, Abigail realized what was happening.

Abigail gasped. "Snips is moving the targets!" she exclaimed.

"Good detective work, Boxcar Bonnie," Lucky said, naming her favorite detective from the books she loved.

Lucky loved to solve a mystery, so Abigail asked, "But how's he doing it?"

Lucky rolled her hands into little circles and peered through as if her fingers were binoculars. "There's a rope tied to each target. The targets are on wheels. My guess is that Snips has Señor Carrots tied to that rope, and he is pulling the targets out of the way. He's moving them slowly enough that if you're watching the arrow, you won't notice!"

Before they could discuss what to do about it, Ms. Hungerford called for the Miradero herd to mount.

Lucky always rode without a saddle, so she waited for the others to check their tack.

"Snips is ruining everything!" complained Abigail. "Boots and Bows is hard enough for Boomerang and me. Now we won't have a chance at all."

"We don't have time to stop him, and we can't reveal that he's here, so we should try to do our best, just like we planned," Pru suggested.

"*Ugh!*" Abigail moaned, but she agreed. "I guess if no one earns a badge, maybe we can convince Ms. Hungerford to let us all try again tomorrow."

"We can use the rope to tie Snips to a tree so he can't pull the targets away," Pru said with a wink.

Normally, Abigail would *probably* protest tying her brother to a tree, but this time, tying him seemed the best option.

"Okay," she said as Lucky swung up on Spirit's back. "Don't feel bad when you miss the targets. Since no one will get the badge today, maybe we can blame the wind or something." It wasn't a good idea—she hated the lie—and now, hiding Snips made two strikes against the value of honesty, but what else could they do?

Lucky nodded. "Come on, Spirit." She leaned over her horse's neck and hugged him tightly. "Since we aren't going to hit any targets anyway, let's ride faster than ever! We'll go down in defeat with style."

She moved with Spirit to the starting block. Pru handed Lucky the quiver of arrows, and she swung the case and strap over her shoulder.

Ms. Hungerford sounded the horn.

Spirit took off at a gallop. Lucky, willing to take an even more daring ride than usual, balanced as she stood up on Spirit's back for the first shot.

"It's too bad about Snips's sabotage," said Abigail when the arrow flew. "That would have been a perfect—"

"Bull's-eye!" Pru exclaimed. Lucky was the first Filly of the day to hit the target dead center.

She hit the next target while leaning off Spirit's side like a trick rider.

"Bull's-eye again!" Pru cheered.

"Bull's-eye?!" Abigail said, more a question than an exclamation.

"Yep," Pru said, softening her cheers.

When she reached the fourth target, Lucky decided to trick things up—she stood on his back backward, leaned down, and shot the arrow between her own legs. The trick shot was amazing and risky.

"And another bull's-eye!" Abigail said with less enthusiasm. Lucky was a great rider, a great shot, and for her—the targets didn't move.

Lucky and Spirit rushed back to where Pru and Abigail were still standing at the starting block.

"Congratulations," Pru said.

"Snips didn't move the targets when I shot at them," Lucky said. "Spirit and I just did what we'd planned all along." She frowned. "I don't get it. What is he up to?"

Pru was next. "Let's see what happens when Chica Linda and I ride through."

Pru had practiced; that was obvious. It wasn't all bull's-eyes like Lucky, but she hit each of the four targets.

Abigail, for all her worry, had an easy time, too.

Boomerang wasn't a fan of arrows or sharp things, and he made his opinion very clear. He was trotting intentionally slowly and barely breathed when Abigail first pulled an arrow from the quiver.

"Four hits," Lucky said when Abigail got through the course.

The Miradero herd's arrows were the only ones that hit the targets all afternoon. The rest of the Fillies did just as poorly as the Golden Valley herd. When the event ended, the only group to earn their badges was the Miradero herd. They were each given the small patch with the arrow embroidered on it.

The girls in the other herds began to complain. There was a rumor going around that the Miradero Fillies had somehow cheated. The other girls wanted a chance to do the Boots and Bows course again.

Ms. Hungerford protested at first, but Abigail knew the passage in the handbook that applied to this situation. She boldly approached Ms. Hungerford. "Ma'am, on page fifty-four of the handbook, it states, 'When badges are not immediately earned, Fillies can be given a second chance in the same weekend event, if the entire group agrees, and there is no foul play involved.'"

"Ah, I see," Ms. Hungerford said, clearly

impressed by Abigail's knowledge. "So the Miradero herd thinks all the Fillies should get a second try?" She looked at all three of them.

"Yes," the PALs replied together.

"Are you certain there was no foul play?" Ms. Hungerford looked hard at Abigail.

"It was the wind," Abigail said, licking her finger and holding it aloft. "Yep, the wind blew when the others shot, but it died down when we took our turn." She swept back her hair, saying, "There it is again, pesky wind."

Olivia gave Abigail a side-eye stare, as if she wasn't buying a word.

Lucky pushed forward to step in front of Abigail. "Since the wind gave us an unfair advantage last time, tell you what: We, the Miradero herd, won't participate again. We already got the badges, so we'll just stand here out of the way."

Pru looked at the clouds and said, "It looks as if the big winds are over now. It's a good time to try again."

Abigail begged, "Please, Ms. Hungerford, let the other Frontier Fillies have a do-over."

Ms. Hungerford thought about it for a long moment, and then she said, "I agree. All Fillies may try again."

As the other herds gathered at the starting gate for the second time, Ms. Hungerford turned her back to the PALs. Abigail, Pru, and Lucky used the opportunity to hurry into the trees where no one would see them.

"Snips!" Abigail whispered, searching for her brother.

He crept out of some camouflage he'd created with leaves. Señor Carrots was with him. A rope, just as they'd expected, was tied from a target to the donkey's saddle. Ropes connected to the other three targets lay on the ground.

"You're welcome," Snips said with a wide grin. "If Miradero is the only herd to win the badges, you'll look so good that you'll earn the shiny trophy, too! It's my most devious plan ever. I'm a genius."

Lucky said, "We'll earn the Heart on our own. Don't ruin this for everyone else!"

"Go back to the tent," Pru said.

"Stay invisible!" Abigail exclaimed.

With a huff, Snips said, "Come on, Señor Carrots, our genius isn't appreciated here. Let us retreat." Guiding the donkey with the rope, they took a few steps away, but then Snips turned back. He shouted, "Wait till you see what I have planned for tomorrow!" With a cackling laugh that bounced around the thick trees, he took off running toward the campsite.

Abigail thought about the next day. "No, thanks." She called out after him, "We don't need your help!"

Her shout was met by more maniacal laughter.

"Don't worry," Lucky told Abigail. "We'll stop him before he tries anything sneaky."

"Snips is tricky," Abigail said. "I should know. He's been tricking me his whole life."

"But now the PALs are watching." Pru turned Chica Linda back toward the course for Boots and Bows.

They got back to the starting gate just as Ana was heading out on Cupcake for her second time at the course. This time she hit every target. Jimena, too. Olivia and Riley and Sophie and all the girls hit at least three targets.

When it was over, Abigail looked out toward where the others were proudly sewing on their new badges. "There are two more badges to earn," she said. "Let's just make sure Snips stays away from the Majestic Mare event tomorrow!"

✿ Diary Entry ✿

Dear Diary,

What am I going to do about Snips? Of all times to become invisible, he picks now! I can't find him anywhere.

Pru and Lucky and I got back to the tent after an amazingly great time at Boots and Bows, and I was ready to face the evil Snips and his donkey sidekick. I was thinking about our mom and dad—what would they do? I can't send him to his room or take away dessert. I can't ban him from riding Señor Carrots. I'm just a kid, so what should I do?

Okay, Abigail, think....

Here's what I can do:

1) Tie him to a tree. That was Pru's idea, and I'm starting to think it's the best idea I've ever heard.

2) Zip him in the tent, but the zipper works both ways. He'll escape.

3) Convince him I don't want to take home the Hungerford Heart. That's a pretty good idea, because if I didn't want it anymore, he wouldn't think he needs to help me get it.

Problem is that I really, really want it. I'm not Maricela. I can't act.

UGH!

4) Here's a long-shot idea: I talk to him. Like, really, really, really talk. I mean, we talked before when I told him to stay invisible, but that didn't work, so now I'll talk more. I'll explain how he's ruining our chance to take home the Hungerford Heart. As I write this down, I think this isn't such a long shot; it's really a good idea. Maybe the

best. I mean, I think I could talk some sense into that brother of mine, and if I can't, maybe Pru or Lucky can. I think that's what we need: a meeting. It's like when adults say they need to talk about "adult things" and go into another room, only we'll talk about "kid things" and go into the tent.

I'll explain to Snips <u>exactly</u> why he has to stay invisible. I'll explain about the Heart and the badges and the handbook and everything. And I'll keep on explaining things to him until he decides to change. I can talk a lot. I might read him parts of the handbook. Even if it takes hours, and I have to talk till my throat hurts, and no one sleeps all night long, I am going to make him understand. When I'm done, he'll be begging to stay in the tent. Talking is my greatest strength, even more than braiding manes and tails. I've got this, and in the end, evil Snips will agree to be a better Snips.

I might have to talk to Señor Carrots, too. If I must, I will. I can be pretty convincing to horses and donkeys—just ask Boomerang.

But first, before I can talk to Snips, I have to make him visible again. And that brings me to my next great idea. The best idea.

Here's what I am going to do to make my brother visible:

5) Lure him out with s'mores.

Gotta run! I'm off to the campfire. S'mores for me. S'mores for Lucky. S'mores for Pru. S'mores for Boomerang. And one very special s'mores trap to catch myself a little brother.

CHAPTER 4

The campfire was fun, but afterward was disappointing.

When Ms. Hungerford put out the fire, Pru, Lucky, and Abigail each saved her last s'more. The plan was to set them out in front of the tent and catch Snips when he came to snack—and since Snips loved snacks, they figured it would be easy to nab him. Then Abigail would talk his ears off until he agreed to stay away during the Majestic Mare event, which was in the grassy field the next morning.

But when they left the campfire, Abigail noticed a trail of graham cracker crumbs that led from the fire pit down the path to the Miradero tent. There was a chocolate smear on the tent flap and sticky marshmallow on the zipper. But no Snips.

These three clues were all Lucky needed to solve the mystery.

She declared that Snips had been to the campfire himself and stolen a treat.

Abigail wasn't willing to give up, and she convinced Pru and Lucky to sit outside for a few hours before they finally gave up and ate the s'mores themselves.

When she couldn't keep her eyes open another second, Abigail crawled into the tent to discover that Snips was already there, snoring soundly. She couldn't figure out how he'd gotten past her, but she wasn't going to wake him up to ask. He looked so peaceful and quiet—this was how she liked Snips the best. She'd just talk to him in the morning. So she crawled into her sleeping bag and settled next to him. Within seconds, she was also sound asleep.

When the sun began to rise, Abigail opened
her heavy eyes to discover Snips sitting up,
staring at her.

"Good morning, my favorite sister," he
whispered, since Lucky and Pru were still
snoozing.

Abigail yawned. "It's too early," she said.
"Not time to wake up yet. Need more sleep."
In the back of her head was the nagging
feeling she needed to talk to Snips, but for
the life of her, she couldn't remember about
what.

"Señor Carrots and I have plans." He
smiled a toothy grin. "Big plans for today. Big,
huge, ginormous plans. It's gonna be the best
day at the Jamboree ever." He pushed back
and undid the zipper of the tent. "So see ya
later, alligator," Snips said cheerfully. "Don't
let the bedbugs bite. A stitch in time saves

nine." He muttered, "I don't even know what that means...." And then he was gone.

A moment later, Abigail closed her eyes against the rays of the rising sun. It felt as if the conversation was a dream. She was so tired. Her eyes began to close again, and her last thought before she fell back asleep was, *I forgot to tell Snips all the reasons he needs to stay invisible....*

"We really have to hurry," Pru said as Abigail gathered her supplies for the Majestic Mare event. They'd slept through breakfast. Pru's stomach rumbled loudly.

"Here." Abigail opened her sleepover sack and threw some horse cookies to Pru and Lucky. "I made these myself. They're hard as rocks, but very nutritious." The cookies were made of oats, berries, and molasses.

Pru nibbled on the side of one, and then she decided she wasn't all that hungry. "I think I'll save this for Chica Linda," she said, putting it in her pocket.

Lucky took a bigger bite. "Oh no! I think I broke a tooth."

Abigail and Pru rushed over to look in her mouth.

"Just kidding," Lucky said, smiling to show her perfectly good teeth. "Spirit's going to love this treat."

Abigail put her own biscuit in her pocket for Boomerang. She apologized to her friends. "Sorry. If we hadn't been up so late, everything would be different." Abigail huffed. "Blast that Snips. He's ruining everything."

"No apology necessary. Today's a new day," Lucky assured her. "The Miradero herd is back on track. First we'll earn the Majestic Mare badge, and then we'll focus on being honorable."

"And valorous," Pru said.

"And compassionate," Lucky said.

"And honest, too," Abigail added as she zipped her small carrying bag. "We've got to fix our honesty problem."

"All of them," Pru assured her. "We'll be the most heartful Fillies in the valley."

"In the *world*," Lucky said, grabbing Abigail's sack. "Now let's go make some pretty horses."

While walking to the horses, Abigail told Lucky and Pru what she had in mind. "I have a rainbow of ribbons," she explained. "All three horses are going to match. We'll start with red ribbons in the tips of their tails, then orange, yellow, green, blue, indigo. If we've done it correctly, moving up inch by inch, we should have violet ribbons at the front of each horse's mane."

"Sounds fancy," Lucky said. "Though I'm not sure that Spirit will go for standing around while I braid his mane."

"He'll do it," Abigail assured her.

"Really?" Lucky frowned. "Spirit has a mind of his own."

"I know," Abigail said. "That's why I explained it to him before we came to the Jamboree." She nodded confidently. "He's agreed."

"Uh, okay," Lucky said with an uncertain glance to Pru. "If you *talked* to him…"

"It's all set," Abigail said. "Chica Linda is ready to be a rainbow of color, too."

Chica Linda didn't usually protest grooming. She liked it. Pru said, "I'm guessing she nodded when you talked to her?"

"Yep," Abigail said. She took her supply bag from Lucky and patted the side. "We're all set."

"Spirit!" Lucky cheered when she saw her mustang. "How are you?" She rubbed her hands over his neck and down toward his belly. "I hear you are ready to be even more majestic." Lucky couldn't read the expression in Spirit's eyes, but she knew that he'd want to make her happy.

"Hiya, Chica Linda," Pru greeted her horse. "We'll start with a quick bath. How's that sound?" Chica Linda whinnied happily.

"Boomerang." Abigail brought her horse around next to the others. "Do you want a cookie?" She fished the hard molasses biscuit out of her pocket and fed it to him. Boomerang ate the whole cookie in one bite. "You must be hungry!" Abigail laughed. "I hope you're full now! We have a busy day."

"Hey." Jimena and her horse, Duchess, approached. "It was fun last night at the campfire." She looked to Pru. "That ghost story you told was really scary."

"It wasn't true, was it?" Ana said. "I mean, there wasn't really a headless horseman riding through Miradero, was there?"

"It was a long time ago," Pru assured them. "I haven't seen him in years."

She gave a sly wink to Lucky, who said, "Not since the headless horsewoman arrived in town."

"On the headless horse," Abigail added.

"You're joking around," Olivia said, leading her own horse over to where they'd gathered.

Pru shrugged but didn't reply.

"Fillies!" Ms. Hungerford called the herds together before anyone else could ask Pru about her story. "Today is the day to show us your best grooming skills. Does anyone know the requirements for the Majestic Mare badge?"

Abigail was the first to raise her hand.

"All right, Abigail," Ms. Hungerford said when no additional hands went up. "Please tell the others what to expect today."

Abigail jumped onto Boomerang's back so she could address the entire group without yelling. "There are three parts to earning this badge," she said, holding up three fingers. "One: bathing your horse beautiful. That means using nice-smelling soap and then scrubbing and washing it all off. Two: grooming with brushes and picks and combs until your horse gleams. And three: making your horse extra majestic."

"Very good, Abigail—" Ms. Hungerford began, but Abigail interrupted.

"I wasn't done. There are three parts to being majestic." Abigail held up three fingers on her other hand. "One: brushing the mane and tail. Two: braiding the mane and tail. And three: decorating the mane and tail with ribbons and bows. There are many different kinds of braids, and I can show you each one if you want. First there's the—"

"Very, very good, Abigail," Ms. Hungerford said approvingly. "It's clear you've read the handbook."

"More like memorized it," Lucky said with a snicker.

A hand shot up from a Filly in the back. "What if we aren't very good at braiding?" Sophie asked. There was a nervous twitch in her voice. "Can we still earn the badge?"

"It's not a competition," Ms. Hungerford reminded the Fillies. "Just do your best."

"See?" Abigail smiled at Pru and Lucky. "That's what I've been saying all along!"

Ms. Hungerford carried out buckets and brushes for the girls and led them to the river to collect water. On this side of the valley, the water ran full and heavy, with a rushing current. The girls were warned to be extra careful when filling their buckets while Ms. Hungerford stood guard to make sure no one fell into the wild stream.

The whole way to the river and back again, Abigail kept her eyes peeled for Snips.

"Could he have gone home?" Pru asked her when they didn't see him lurking anywhere.

"No chance," Lucky said. "But, hopefully, he's decided that it's better to stay hidden."

Abigail pinched her lips together. Not seeing her brother made her a little worried about him, but she'd still rather not see him than see him.

Washing the horses was a ton of fun. The Fillies got into it and helped one another. When Sophie's horse kicked over the water bucket, Lucky and Pru gave her some of their water. Ms. Hungerford had brought lavender-scented shampoo for the horses, and they smelled amazing.

"Spirit loves a good bath," Lucky said, pouring water over his back. His coat shone in the sunlight.

Chica Linda waited until Pru had made the soap into big, lush bubbles, then shook her head, throwing bubbles from her neck into Pru's hair.

Jimena offered to help, tossing a handful of water at Pru. The water landed *splat*, right on top of Pru's head, and dripped down her back and shoulders. At first, Pru looked as if she might be mad, but then she said, "Hey, thanks for washing the soap out," and she shook her head and whinnied just like Chica Linda.

The Fillies laughed and played as they cleaned the horses' hooves, used curry combs to remove dirt from their bodies, and smoothed their coats with dandy brushes.

"It's majestic time!" Abigail told Pru and Lucky as she excitedly opened her supply bag. Ms. Hungerford had brought long ribbons and colored yarn for the girls who didn't have their own ribbon and bows. She put her box down in the middle of everyone, while Abigail put her bag near Spirit, Boomerang, and Chica Linda.

Everyone was having fun. Abigail checked to see what Sophie was doing, since she had

been worried this wasn't her best event.
Sophie had made little braids in her horse's
tail. They weren't woven with ribbons, but
that was okay. Abigail might suggest that
Sophie should tie a bow around its tail when
the braids were complete, and then it would
be perfectly majestic.

Other Fillies were braiding long pieces of
ribbon into their horses' manes and tails. It
was like a beauty shop for horses, and Abigail
was having the best time ever. She loved
turning Boomerang into a majestic-looking
horse and was sure everything was on track
for them to really *earn* their first badge of the
weekend.

She'd just started her first braid when
suddenly an odd, high-pitched voice came
from down by the raging river.

"Help!" the voice squeaked.

"Did you hear that?" Ana asked the PALs.

"You don't think…?" Abigail dropped her ribbons and bows and started to run. "Could Snips be in trouble?" she asked Pru and Lucky as they headed out after her.

The other girls left their half-majestic horses and followed.

"Hello?" Abigail called out at the riverbank. "Anyone there?"

It was silent. Like good Fillies, the herds fanned out and searched the riverbanks. There was no one there. Eventually, they all started to doubt that they'd even heard a voice at all.

"Back to camp, Fillies," Ms. Hungerford instructed the girls. "It must have been the wind in the trees."

When they arrived at the field, everything was a mess. The ribbons that the Fillies had been using to make their horses majestic and pretty were now torn and dirty, scattered all over the ground. There were only a few clean ribbons left, and those belonged to the Miradero herd.

"What happened here?" Ms. Hungerford said, not really expecting an answer.

Abigail breathed heavily and frowned. She whispered to Lucky and Pru, "Looks as if Snips has struck again. He distracted us all so he could make this mess."

"That Snips!" Lucky exclaimed. "He still thinks we need his help. He messed up everyone else's ribbons but left ours. That way we'd get the badge and no one else would!"

"He is so tricky," Abigail moaned, looking around at the girls and their horses.

Jimena said, "This is horrible." She picked up a massive tangle of bows and ribbons.

All the herds worked together to unwind the ribbons and salvage the few pieces that hadn't been ruined. When they were done,

Ms. Hungerford said, "Our next activity will begin in twenty minutes. You must finish the requirements for this badge before then."

A cry of "Oh no!" rose from the Fillies. There wasn't enough time to do everything again, and they didn't have enough supplies, either!

Abigail looked out at all the plain-looking animals. Since the PALs were the only ones with a full box of clean majestic-making supplies, she told Pru and Lucky, "I think we should help."

"Of course we will!" Lucky said.

"You don't even have to ask me," Pru told them both. "I'm in."

For the next twenty minutes, Abigail braided more manes and tails than she'd ever done before. Pru cut their own ribbons into smaller pieces so there were enough to go around. Lucky tied bows.

The Fillies all helped one another. No one stuck to her own horse. Any horse without a bow got a bow or two. Any horse without braids got braids. And when Ms. Hungerford announced time was up, the Frontier Fillies had a stable of the most majestic horses anyone had ever seen.

A great cheer rose up from the girls when Ms. Hungerford approached holding a bag of badges. She officially inspected each horse before giving its Filly a badge.

When it came time for Boomerang's review, Abigail realized something terrible: The Miradero horses weren't fancy—they were just regular ol' horses.

She tried to explain to Ms. Hungerford. "Pru, Lucky, and I were so busy helping the other Fillies and their horses, we forgot to make our own into Majestic Mares!"

It was true. They'd forgotten to braid their

own horses' manes and tails and tie the planned rainbow of ribbons.

"I'm so sorry, girls," Ms. Hungerford told them. "The handbook rules cannot be bent. Your horses didn't meet the last of the three rules."

Abigail groaned sadly. "They aren't majestic."

Lucky was going to argue, but Abigail raised a hand. "No, stop," she begged.

The other Fillies had already moved on to the next activity, so no one was there to argue for a do-over, like before. This time, the event was over-over.

"Are you sure?" Pru whispered to Abigail. "No more arguing about it?"

"We had fun," she said, raising her chin, "but rules are rules, and no one believes in the handbook as much as I do. We didn't earn the badge."

Diary Entry

Dear Diary,

I can't believe this is happening.

Without that badge, we'll never get the votes for the Hungerford Heart. I know, I know...that's not how it works, but seriously, who's going to vote for the herd who can't even make a horse beautiful?

I'm so sad. I want to go home. I even started packing.

Lucky stopped me. She said that we could go home if I really wanted to, but she also reminded me there were

still a trail ride and the big showcase.
We should have fun at the Jamboree.
She also really wants the Saddle
Showcase badge, and so does Pru, so
we shouldn't leave.

Pru reminded me that you didn't
have to earn all the badges to be
in the running to get votes for the
Hungerford Heart.

But I know it helps! A lot! No
one will vote for a herd who didn't get
a badge. Especially one as easy to
earn as the Majestic Mare badge!

After a whole minute of deep
thinking, I decided to stay and was
unpacking when Snips stuck his head
in the tent. He blamed Lucky and
Pru and me for messing up his plans.

Then Snips announced that we'd get our badges tomorrow for certain. He ran away before I could say anything.

Lucky tried to grab his foot to stop him, but she missed. He rolled out of the tent and dashed away, shouting something about how the trophy would be coming to Miradero whether we liked it or not.

I am so mad at Snips for ruining everything, but I'm not giving up. Maybe Pru and Lucky are right, and we can still get the votes for the Heart. We just need to be the most virtuous herd at the Jamboree.

The rest of the day is going to be great. We are going on a trail ride. No badges to earn. A quiet ride will help me think about how we can prove ourselves honorable, compassionate, and valorous. (I'll work on honesty later—Snips is a big problem for that one.) It's just me, Boomerang, our old friends, and our new friends going on a ride around the valley and down by the river.

I can't wait.

And the best part about it is, since it's not a badge or competition, Snips won't think he should "help."

CHAPTER 5

Abigail was riding behind Lucky, who was behind Pru. In front of Pru was the Golden Valley herd. They got to go first, of course, because they were the keepers of the Hungerford Heart. Abigail was jealous, but she didn't let it stick to her. She threw that jealousy in the river and kept riding.

Behind Miradero were the other herds. The horses had all become really friendly and were riding close together. Usually it was best to keep one horse length between riders, but no one was worried about the horses.

Abigail took a quick moment to scan the trees for Snips. Certain that he wasn't around, she relaxed into the ride. It wasn't a great adventure, but it was fun.

They clopped along the river under large trees.

"Duck," Lucky told Abigail as they passed under a thick, low tree branch. She leaned in close to Boomerang's neck as they safely passed under the tree.

"Watch the ground," Pru called out as the horses had to step over a moss-covered fallen log.

Straight up ahead was another low tree branch, and this time, Jimena, since she was in the lead, called out to the herds, "Duck!" She bent low—and then screamed.

From where she was in the line, Abigail couldn't see what had happened. But she could guess. Even a few horses back in the line, Abigail saw Jimena sway to the side in her saddle and struggle to sit straight up.

"Lucky," Abigail said, pointing at Jimena. "I think she bumped her head on the tree branch."

Then suddenly, Olivia, who was behind Jimena, screamed, "Snake!" She pointed to the tree branch but managed to avoid the branch and not hit her head.

The path was narrow, and the horses were bunched up, but as they heard the scream, they reared back, knocking into the horses behind them. Abigail was having a hard time controlling Boomerang, who was scared. There was nowhere to go. The rushing river was to the left and thick trees to the right. The path was tight with horses.

"Don't let your horses bolt," Pru warned the other Fillies. "Hold the reins tightly."

"If the horses run into the water, they might get hurt. And the trees are too tightly woven together," Lucky said. "Stay on the path."

The horses began to settle at the back of

the line, and Abigail breathed a sigh of relief. Things weren't so dangerous if the horses stopped, but if one took off...

Jimena screamed as her horse spooked again and started running—under branches, over logs, down the path. Abigail could see Jimena clutching her forehead as she bounced in the saddle.

"This is not good!" she told Lucky and Pru.

Ms. Hungerford was at the back of the line of horses. Abigail heard her shout, "Oh dear!" but there wasn't a lot she could do. She was too far away from Jimena and Duchess.

Abigail knew only three riders who were close enough to the front and fast enough to save the day.

She shouted, "PALs!"

Pru and Lucky replied, "We're on it!" and the three of them moved their horses off the path and into the river.

They didn't have to go far—just around the rest of the Golden Valley herd—then they'd get back on the path.

The water was rushing, but it was flowing downstream, so they didn't have to fight the current.

Boomerang was a good swimmer, but Spirit was better. They fought their way toward the center of the river. Chica Linda held closer to the shoreline where the water was shallower.

Once back on the narrow path, the PALs spurred their horses to catch Jimena and Duchess.

"Duck!" Lucky was in front. She called out dangers so they would all avoid hitting their heads on branches.

"Log!" Lucky called again as Spirit jumped over a fallen tree. Boomerang and Chica Linda followed Spirit.

Under and over branches and logs they went, speeding to catch up with the runaway horse and its injured rider.

"Jimena!" Abigail called out as they got close. Here the path was wider and the horses could fit side by side. She could see a small cut on Jimena's head. "Can you stop? Pull the reins?"

"I've been trying. Duchess is so scared from the snake, she won't listen."

Abigail was worried that Jimena looked pale and kept leaning back in her saddle. They had to get her off the speeding horse before she fell.

Abigail called to Lucky. "Can you grab Jimena?"

Lucky pulled Spirit to one side of Duchess, while Chica Linda edged onto the other side.

"On the count of three," Lucky told Jimena,

"I need you to jump from your horse to mine. I'll catch you."

Jimena looked doubtful.

"Okay, new plan," Lucky said, not willing to risk it if Jimena didn't want to leap off her horse.

"We're coming to a big ditch up ahead," Pru warned. "Does Duchess know how to jump?"

"No!" Jimena shook her head. "She's new to the arena. I haven't trained her for that yet. And she's so scared, I don't know what she'll do!"

"Okay," Lucky said. "I'm coming over." In a flash, she leaped from Spirit onto Duchess's back, settling behind Jimena in her saddle. "We're going to let Duchess jump the ditch," she told Jimena. Lucky wrapped her arms around Jimena to take the reins.

"I'm scared," Jimena admitted.

Abigail and Boomerang went to the side of

Duchess. Since the horse had never jumped like this before, Boomerang, Spirit, and Chica Linda were all going to show her how to cross the ditch.

The PALs made the count together. "One, two, three—" Boomerang went first, then Chica Linda. Duchess made a perfect landing, and Spirit followed them all across. The girls slowed, stopping just as Ms. Hungerford caught up.

"Oh, Jimena," she said. "I was worried. Let me see your head...."

While Ms. Hungerford helped Jimena, Pru told Abigail, "We did a good job!"

"Yes, we did," Abigail said. Then she leaned down to kiss Boomerang on the neck. "You did well, too."

A few minutes later, all the herds gathered around. They were concerned about Jimena, worried about Duchess, and curious about what had happened back on the trail.

"A snake fell from the tree," Olivia said. "Jimena saw it first and was so scared she forgot to duck. She hit her head on the tree branch, then the snake scared Duchess. I saw the snake, too, but I wasn't scared. My horse is really brave."

Abigail pressed her lips together and said nothing. There was one person she knew who really loved snakes. Could Snips have sabotaged their trail ride?

All the way back, Abigail, Pru, and Lucky rode in silence, and by the time they reached the campsite, Abigail was so sure that he'd dropped the snake, she was too mad to talk.

✿ Diary Entry ✿

Dear Diary,

Snips swears it wasn't him.

I told him the prank was not funny. Funny is when a clown gets hit with a pie in the face or anything involving a rubber chicken.... This was not funny.

Snips promised that he and Señor Carrots had been busy making plans for something else, and that he was nowhere near the trail ride.

I asked for proof.

He refused to tell me what he had been up to.

I demanded he tell me.

He told me that Señor Carrots could prove he wasn't there. I asked how. He said I had to ask Señor Carrots.

<u>AUGH!</u>

I'm supposed to ask a donkey where he was an hour ago? Donkeys have <u>terrible</u> memories!

I have to believe Snips for now. Thing is, I don't think he'd hurt anyone on purpose. Fingers triple crossed I'm right.

I told Snips that he'd better not plan anything to do at tomorrow's Saddle Showcase event.

It's the big last-day celebration and the last chance to earn a badge. Right after the Showcase, all the herds will get to vote. He'd better not ruin that!

Snips just laughed and ran away.

For the Showcase, you can do anything you think of. And I mean anything!

You can slowly ride around the stage area a few times or do tricks or go crazy and put on a big show. Pru is doing the "go crazy" one. She's got a routine where she and Chica Linda perform to music. Lucky is planning to do some tricks. And I'm going to show off Boomerang's barrel-racing skills. And everyone in Miradero knows that Boomerang has some really amazing barrel skills. He rides around them fast, kinda as if his tail were on fire (which was true one time...but let's not talk about that now).

Just as Ms. Hungerford told us to, I've laid out my complete uniform to wear in the morning and am super ready to go.

The Fillies wear: long pants, a crisp white shirt, a neckerchief, a leaf-shaped hat, and a sash with the badges sewn on. I saw some of the other herds sewing on their newly earned badges last night. I tried not to feel bad that the Miradero herd didn't have a Majestic Mare badge to sew on, but I kind of feel as if it's my fault that we didn't get it.

Lucky and Pru are being really nice about everything. Pru says it was Snips's fault we didn't get the Majestic Mare badge. Lucky said that we're having a really good time, and that is what is important.

I'm so mad at Snips for ruining the day that my stomach feels as if there's a rock inside.

He thinks he's helping, but he's not. I'd even give back my Boots and Bows badge and forget about the Saddle Showcase badge if we had a chance at the Hungerford Heart.

But I'm afraid we don't.

CHAPTER 6

It's time to get ready," Ms. Hungerford announced at the end of breakfast. It was a pajama breakfast, so no one was wearing her uniform yet. Abigail discovered, as she asked around, that the other girls had all done exactly the same as the PALs. Their uniforms were laid out and ready to wear. There was so much excitement in the air.

When it was time to go change and get ready, Abigail grabbed a couple of rolls and some juice for Snips, then found Pru and Lucky.

They walked to the tent area together. Their uniforms were where they'd left them, and they all began to get dressed.

This was the last day. After the show,

there was lunch, then voting, and finally the announcement of the Hungerford Heart winner.

"We can't mess up. This is our last chance to earn a badge—" Abigail was saying when suddenly, there was screaming from the other side of camp.

The PALs took off running toward the noise. Abigail's uniform was untucked and her Fillies leaf hat flopped on her head. Lucky was half-dressed, and Pru was ready except for her hat.

"What's going on?" Pru wondered. "That scream sounded terrible."

They hurried past the campfire pit to Jimena's tent, where all the herds had gathered.

"What's up?" Abigail asked. She looked around. Everyone was still wearing pajamas. No one was in uniform. And Jimena was flushed with anger.

"Why did you do it?!" Jimena faced the PALs. She'd been so friendly lately, Abigail wasn't sure what happened. "You're the only ones who would've done it."

"We're like Boxcar Bonnie, solving a mystery," Riley said.

Lucky gasped. "You read Boxcar Bonnie?"

"I do," Riley said in an accusatory tone. "And I have this mystery all figured out!"

"We think you're cheating to win the Hungerford Heart," Olivia announced. "We know you want it."

"I do," Abigail admitted to her, "but it's impossible to cheat to get it. The votes are secret and protected. Only Ms. Hungerford has the paper slips."

"Even if there were a way, which there isn't, we aren't cheaters," Pru insisted.

"We don't know what's even going on," Lucky said, motioning at the other Fillies.

"Ha," Olivia said. "That's what cheaters say." She pointed at the PALs, one at a time, and asked, "How come you are the only ones who have your uniforms, and the rest of us can't find ours?"

"None of you?" Lucky asked, looking at all the herds. "No one has a uniform?"

"No," Jimena confirmed. "And as you know"—she glared at Abigail—"we can't get the badge if we aren't dressed correctly."

"I see...." Abigail took a deep breath.

Ms. Hungerford approached. "What's this I hear about the Miradero herd cheating?" she asked, noticing that Miradero was mostly dressed in uniforms and the other girls were still in their pajamas.

"It makes perfect sense," Jimena said. "They've been causing trouble since the moment they tried to take our camping space."

"That was a misunderstanding," Pru protested.

"Then there was the food fight," Olivia said. "You started it, so you had to clean it up."

"That's not what happened—" Lucky started, but Sophie from the Copper Point herd jumped in.

"The targets were moving at the Boots and Bows," Sophie said. "I saw it!"

"We'd hoped no one noticed that," Abigail said with a grimace.

"So you admit they moved?" Ms. Hungerford asked. She was frowning.

"Yes. But it's not what you think—" Pru began when another girl named Cassie cut in.

"And at the Majestic Mare event, their ribbons were the only ones that didn't get ruined," Cassie said.

"I know," Abigail said, "but that wasn't our fault. You see—"

Jimena touched the sore spot on her head and said, "I bet you put the snake in that tree."

"How would we have done that?" Lucky was getting defensive. "None of this is our fault." She reminded Jimena, "We were behind you. We saved you."

"Yeah, but I think you spooked me and then saved me," Jimena said.

"No. That doesn't make any sense!" Abigail told Jimena. "Why would we do that?"

Jimena thought for a second, and then she said, "I know! You were going to prove that you deserve *our* Hungerford Heart."

"It's not *yours*." Lucky stepped forward.

"See?" Jimena looked to Ms. Hungerford. "They want the Heart more than anything. So they took our uniforms."

"What are you talking about?!" Pru countered. "We need your votes to get the Heart. If we messed things up, we'd never get the Heart."

Abigail was sad, sadder than ever before.

She said, "It's all ruined. No one will vote for us now." Her voice choked as she said, "The Jamboree is almost over and everything is so messed up." She looked at all the other girls and said, "Do you want to know the truth?"

They all did.

Ms. Hungerford said, "Please explain, Abigail."

She took another breath and barreled into the story. "My little brother, Snips, followed us here and has been messing up things all along. Lucky, Pru, and I—we've been trying to fix the messes he's making!"

At first no one believed them, but Abigail, Pru, and Lucky took turns explaining how Snips started the food fight, moved the targets, and tangled up the ribbons and bows.

"Did he spook Duchess?" Jimena asked, touching her sore head.

"No, that was a snake," Abigail said. "I'm,

like, ninety-eight percent sure. Maybe ninety-seven, but no less than ninety-five percent sure it wasn't his idea."

Once they'd finally come clean with it all, Ms. Hungerford asked, "Where is your brother now?"

"I don't know." Abigail shrugged. "But when we find him, I'm guessing that we'll find your uniforms, too." She felt as if she had to add, "He isn't *all* bad. Snips thought he was helping us."

"It was wrong not to tell me your brother was here all along," Ms. Hungerford said. "Abigail, you should have been honest at the Jamboree's start and not now, at the end."

Abigail frowned. "I'm sorry," she said.

Lucky and Pru apologized, too.

A small voice came from the top of a nearby tree. "I'm sorry, too," the voice said.

Then from high in the tree, Frontier Fillies uniforms began to fall to the ground like rain.

119

Diary Entry

Dear Diary,

Snips climbed down from the tree and apologized for all the trouble he'd caused. He'd been listening to Jimena and the others get mad at Pru, Lucky, and me and felt bad. Well, bad in a Snips way. He was like, "Sorry, but if you'd done it my way, you'd have three badges and the Hungerford Heart, too. But since you won't listen to your smartest brother, I guess I apologize for you not listening."

So, it wasn't exactly an apology, but I'll take it.

Ms. Hungerford was mad and yet pretty nice about it all, too. She said she was glad that we finally told her what was going on, but she repeated that we should have said something earlier. She'd have found an escort to take Snips home. It didn't have to be me. I guess I should have thought that maybe she knew people in the nearby town, but I didn't really think of asking for help. I just assumed I could handle my brother. I should have known better.

When I told her that I had been trying (with Pru and Lucky) to get him to stay invisible the whole time, Ms. Hungerford said the most shocking thing ever.

She said, "Since you've been cleaning up his messes all along, you should be the ones to clean up this last mess, too." Then she told everyone that the Miradero herd was going to determine what to do with Snips!

Us? We're kids! But she said that we'd shown "resourcefulness in countering his sabotage," so we should finish it all up.

She also said that, as our punishment, we couldn't participate in the Saddle Showdown.

My friends were great about it. Since we couldn't ride and would never get the badge (or the Heart), I suggested that we go back to Miradero early. We probably should have left last time when they convinced me to stay. Pru and Lucky said they wanted to stick around and cheer on our new friends (even if they still might be a little mad at us). Yeah, they convinced me again.

I've been thinking about what Ms. Hungerford said about us having to figure out what to do with Snips, and I have an idea. If we stay, then Snips stays. I think I have a way to lock him in the tent, where he should have been the whole time.

To make sure he stays put, we'll move our tent near the Showcase, where Lucky and Pru and I can guard

Snips and watch our friends do the show at the same time. Señor Carrots can watch the show with us since he's really an innocent donkey in Snips's trickery. After Ms. Hungerford officially gives Golden Valley the Hungerford Heart (again), we can pack up to go home.

Snips can't ruin anything else for us because from here on, he will be invisible!

PS: If I could add one thing to my plan, I'd invite Mary Pat and Bianca to stay in the tent with him. Ha.

CHAPTER 7

The herds gave amazing performances. Jimena and Golden Valley played Simon Says, with the other horses imitating what Jimena and Duchess did. It was really funny.

The Battersea herd rolled giant hoops while riding their horses.

Sophie stood on her horse's back and read poetry.

Cassie's horse took a bow after catching carrots in the air. (Boomerang would have been good at that one, too.)

When it was all over, everyone gathered for their badges.

Abigail, Lucky, and Pru cheered the loudest

as all the herds got their Saddle Showdown badges.

Right after the badges, the Fillies got to vote for the herd they thought should take home the Hungerford Heart. There was no question in Abigail's mind who deserved it. She put her ballot in the box, feeling proud and satisfied.

Ms. Hungerford then asked the Golden Valley herd to bring the Hungerford Heart trophy forward. It was the moment Abigail had most been waiting for the entire weekend.

Even though they were no longer in the running for it, Abigail felt her heart race, just seeing the finely crafted silver trophy again.

"I'm so glad your herd will get the Heart again this year," Abigail whispered to Jimena. She winked. "But we'll try again next year if that's okay."

"We'd love that…" Jimena said in a loud voice.

Ms. Hungerford stood in front of all the herds. She held the trophy high, so everyone could see it, and announced: "This year the Hungerford Heart goes to the herd from Miradero!"

"Huh?" Abigail wasn't sure she'd heard that right.

"You don't have to wait for next year!" Jimena handed her the trophy. "We all voted for you." She pointed to every girl at the Jamboree. "We all think that you deserve the prize for showing the best Frontier Filly values." She reviewed the weekend. "You showed honor by standing up and taking the blame for the food fight. You fought for us all to get another chance at Boots and Bows, which showed valor. You were honest when you finally told us about Snips." She gave a side-eye to the tent where Abigail's brother was peeking his head through the flap. He waved sheepishly.

"What about compassion?" Lucky said. "I don't think we've—"

Abigail poked her. "Don't talk them out of it!"

Ms. Hungerford finished for Jimena. "You showed compassion toward Snips when you all decided not to send him home...or tie him to a tree." She laughed. "Pru told me that was one of your ideas."

"One of our best ideas." Pru shrugged. "But not practical."

"You showed restraint and great care for your brother when you could have acted in frustration and anger." Ms. Hungerford put her hand on Abigail's shoulder. "That's what compassion is."

Abigail took a deep breath and let herself take the trophy from Jimena.

"You also saved me when my horse ran away," Jimena said. "I'll never forget it. Thanks."

Lucky and Pru gathered with the Fillies,

as did Snips, who slipped out of the tent and squeezed among the Fillies for a front-row view.

"*Ha!*" Snips said with a cheer. "I knew it. I told you I'd help you win the trophy, and I did."

Lucky quickly put her hand over Snips's mouth while Pru held his arms.

"It's okay," Abigail said. "We know he didn't help us. It doesn't matter what he thinks."

Pru and Lucky let him go. Abigail said, "Snips, we will talk about this more on the way home." She sounded very motherly. "Go pack up Señor Carrots."

"Aw shucks," Snips said. "I want to stay at Camp Jamboree forever."

Abigail narrowed her eyes at him and threatened, "I swear, Snips, my Frontier Filly compassion is slipping away. If you don't get out of here now, I'll have to give back the trophy." She didn't say what she'd do to him, but her eyes were really scary.

"I'm going." Snips sulked off toward their tent area. "Good-bye, fellow Fillies! It's been fun knowing ya. See you at the next Jamboree."

"That will never happen." Abigail rolled her eyes as he walked away.

"I guess we should go pack up, too," Pru told Lucky and Abigail.

"One more thing…" Ms. Hungerford stopped them from leaving. "I believe we owe you these." In her hand were the badges each girl had missed: Majestic Mare and Saddle Showdown.

Abigail looked at the badges, then stepped closer to Pru and Lucky. They whispered to one another for a long moment, then Abigail moved back to Ms. Hungerford.

"We didn't earn them," she told their leader.

Ms. Hungerford said, "It's not your fault that Snips made the tasks difficult for you."

"While that's true," Lucky said, "we respectfully do not accept the badges."

Pru explained, "We want to come back next year! We can earn them then."

"Wait! You can still earn them now!" Jimena said. "Remember that rule in the handbook that says, 'When badges are not immediately earned, Fillies can be given a second chance in the same weekend event, if the entire group agrees and there is no foul play involved'?"

"The rule on page fifty-four?" Abigail asked. She began to smile.

"We all want Miradero to have another chance!" Jimena said. "The weekend isn't over yet."

Very slowly, Ms. Hungerford began to smile. "I suppose there is time left," she said.

Abigail sat on Boomerang's back waiting for the horn. Boomerang was groomed with ribbons that made his mane and tail look like a rainbow. Chica Linda and Spirit wore matching rainbows.

The PALs had earned the Majestic Mare badges, and now Abigail was going to ride fast in her Saddle Showcase performance. Her original idea had been to gallop around barrels, which was one of her and Boomerang's best skills, but they didn't have barrels at the campsite. Instead, Lucky and Pru were sitting on their horses in spots the barrels would have been. She was going to ride around them in a figure-eight pattern.

When Ms. Hungerford blew the horn, Boomerang took off. Abigail lay close to his neck as they rounded Lucky and Spirit.

"Atta girl!" Lucky cheered.

"Go, go, go!" Pru called out as Boomerang and Abigail flew around them.

There was a cheer from the Fillies. Snips

was in the middle of the herds, frowning, while Señor Carrots stood by the fence nearby.

Jimena shouted, "That's probably a world record for the fastest barrel race without barrels!"

Abigail laughed, and then she and Boomerang went to the center of the field area and took a quick bow.

Lucky was up next. She hung off Spirit's side and then swung up onto his back with a twist and a half flip. Abigail didn't even know that Lucky'd been working on a cartwheel, which she did on Spirit's backside as he raced forward. She also managed a somersault down Spirit's back and a flip to dismount. It was amazing. When Lucky took a bow, the herds went wild.

Pru's routine was based on a competition form she did called dressage. In dressage, Chica Linda would prance to music in a very specific pattern. Again, since they weren't actually competing, she decided to ratchet it up and try things she'd never done before. Since she didn't have a way to play music, Pru handed out lyrics to one of the Fillies' anthems. Everyone sang while Chica Linda danced around, her hooves moving in rhythm to the beat. It was great, and when she finished, she got a standing ovation.

❀ Diary Entry ❀

Dear Diary,

We just got home from the Frontier Fillies Jamboree.

When I told Mom and Dad about Snips and everything he'd done all weekend, they escorted him right away to his room and told him that he would be grounded for a good, long while. I could hear him yelling, "How can I be grounded? I helped them!" all the way down the hall.

I was happy to let them take over

Snips for a while. I had other things to worry about.

I met Lucky and Pru at the barn where they were settling in Chica Linda and Spirit for the night. I brought apples for Boomerang and the others.

We fed the horses apples and started talking about next year's Jamboree.

Ms. Hungerford told us that there'd be three new badges to earn, but she wouldn't tell us what they are, so we can't practice. That's okay. I have a big surprise for everyone myself.

I am going to make the horses "uniforms" just like the ones we wear as Fillies. They need leaf hats like ours.

Wouldn't that be cute? I was thinking I could also make sashes, and then we could have badges that the horses earn, just like we do. Then we could sew them on, and the horses could parade around in their hats and sashes, and then it would be extra cute.

I have a whole year, so I'll make them for everyone. Wouldn't Duchess and Cupcake and all the others love horse uniforms, too?

I was thinking of fun horse badge ideas—for horses, not horse badges for people—while I was putting away the tack. I was surprised when I found a note in my saddlebag. It was from Jimena.

It said:

> Miradero, take a bow....
> The Hungerford Heart is
> yours...for now.

I giggled and set the Heart on a shelf in the barn. It glistened in the early evening sunset. I was so proud. I was going to polish the metal and oil the wood base every day until next year's Frontier Fillies Jamboree.

I blew a kiss to the Hungerford Heart, and then Pru said, "Hey, Abigail, tell us all about the Heart."

So I did.

"The trophy itself is a metal sculpture forged in the blacksmith shop where Ms. Hungerford's father worked as a boy. It's rumored that she forged the metal herself, heating and pounding a long silver bar and then bending it into the shape of a perfectly proportioned heart.

"The statue represents the Heart of the Fillies and sits on a cherrywood base that is said to come from the very same tree as President George Washington's teeth. Engraved in the base are the four noble virtues of the truest Frontier Filly.

"You know, the Hungerford Heart is named for Ms. Hungerford's grandmother...."

Turn the page for a sneak peek at the adventure that started it all

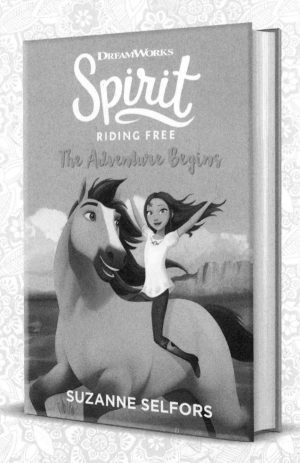

Introduction

A buckskin stallion stood at the edge of his herd, his head held high, his eyes alert. While the other horses filled their bellies with tender spring grass, his gaze swept the prairie. Leaves rustled in the breeze. Butterflies flitted among stalks of milkweed. A toad leaped onto a rock, to bask in the morning sun.

All appeared peaceful.

The stallion sniffed the air for hidden signs of danger. No damp scent of wolf. No musky scent of bear. And no people, with their strange odors of fire and soap. His ears pricked, listening for anything that might cause trouble, but he was greeted with a gentle trickle from a nearby creek and the lazy whistle of a meadowlark as it called to its mate. The stallion nodded with contentment.

He lowered his head and nibbled the sweet grass, his tail flicking once, twice, to chase away a dragonfly. But on this morning, grazing wasn't on his mind. He lifted his head again, his legs stiffening. The prairie stretched before him, a vast, wide-open space, and it was calling. He stomped his hoof and snorted. The others understood, for he was young and restless. They stepped aside. His sister gazed at him. *Go*, her eyes said. Checking once more to make sure the herd was safe, he took a deep breath. Then he reared up and...

...charged!

Nothing stood in his way. No mountains, no rivers, no houses or train tracks. With his face in the wind, he was filled with immeasurable joy. He was free.

The morning sun warmed the prairie as the stallion's galloping hooves beat their wild rhythm.

1

The morning sun streamed through the windows as Lucky's shoes beat their wild rhythm.

Though Lucky was a natural runner, with long, strong legs, the shoes themselves hadn't been designed for such activity. Made from stiff black leather, with a half-inch heel, they laced tightly up the shins. That very morning the boots had been polished to a perfect sheen by the family butler. If she kept running, Lucky would surely develop blisters, but she didn't have far to go.

With no one around to witness, Lucky picked up speed and darted down the hallway of Madame Barrow's Finishing School for Young Ladies. Running within school walls was strictly prohibited, along with other disrespectful activities like pencil gnawing and gum chewing. But sometimes rules had to be broken, especially when a hot, buttered scone was at stake. So Lucky ran as fast as she could, her long brown braid thumping against her back. Morning tea at Barrow's was a tradition the headmistress had brought with her from England. The school's cook could make the pastry so flaky it practically melted in the mouth. And she stuffed each one with a huge dollop of salted butter and sweet blackberry jam. Lucky's mouth watered just thinking about it. But she was late. So very late. Which wasn't entirely her fault.

There'd been a...*distraction*.

She'd been looking out the window as she tended to do during morning recitations, her mouth moving automatically, for she knew her multiplication tables by heart. "Twelve times five is sixty. Twelve times six is seventy-two." Her legs felt twitchy, as they often did when she was forced to sit for long periods of time. "Twelve times seven is eighty-four. Twelve times eight is ninety-six."

"Lucky, please stop fiddling," the teacher said.

"Yes, ma'am." Lucky sat up straight and tucked her feet behind the chair legs to keep them still.

"Continue, everyone."

"Twelve times nine is—"

Lucky stopped reciting. Something on the other side of the street caught her eye. It was a horse, but not the usual sort that one saw in the city. This horse wasn't attached to a carriage or wagon. A bright-red blanket lay across his back and feathers hung from his black mane. He was being led down the sidewalk by a man whose long blond hair was topped by a cowboy hat. The fringe on the man's pants jiggled as he walked. Certainly the city was full of colorful people who came from every corner of the world, but Lucky had never seen a cowboy in person, only in photographs. He walked in a funny, bowlegged way and was handing out pieces of paper to passersby. Lucky leaned closer to the window, but a carriage pulled up and blocked her view.

"Twelve times fourteen is..." Lucky tapped her fingers on the desk. She couldn't get that cowboy and his beautiful horse out of her mind. What were they doing in the city?

"Lucky. Please sit still!"

And so it was that after recitations, instead of heading to tea with the other students, Lucky snuck out the front door to see if the cowboy was still there.

He wasn't. And by that time, morning tea had already begun.

The headmistress believed that teatime was as crucial to a young lady's education as literature or history because it taught manners and the important art of conversation. Plus, she insisted that the tea they served at Barrow's Finishing School was superior because it came all the way from England and had a picture of Queen Victoria on the tin. Lucky wasn't a huge fan of the stuff, but those scones were to die for.

She bounded up the flight of stairs, lifting her long skirt so she wouldn't get tangled. She detested the school uniform—a stiff white blouse that buttoned all the way to the chin and a gray wool skirt that always seemed too heavy and too hot. She'd pleaded many times for a change in uniform. She'd brought in newspaper articles to show the headmistress that pants were all the rage in other countries. But her reasonable request fell on deaf ears, for the headmistress was as immobile as a ship in the sand. "My young ladies will not be seen in public in a pair of bloomers!"

Lucky leaped onto the second-floor landing. From the end of the hall came the clinking of china and the quiet conversations of her fellow students. She was almost there. Still gripping her skirt, she dashed out of the stairwell, turned sharply on her heels, and then raced down the hall.

Only to bump into something.

Correction—into *someone*.

When a scone-craving, restless student collides with a no-nonsense, uppity headmistress, the impact is the stuff of legend. Not only was the wind knocked out of both parties, but they were thrown off-balance. Objects flew into the air—a notebook, a hair comb, a marble pen. When Lucky reached out to break her fall, she grabbed the first thing in front of her, which happened to be the headmistress's arm. Down they both tumbled, landing on the hallway carpet in a most unladylike way. Lucky knew this was bad—very bad. The headmistress had probably never sat on the ground in her entire life, let alone been knocked down to it!

Madame Barrow pushed a stray lock of hair from her eyes. "Fortuna. Esperanza. Navarro. Prescott!" she said between clenched teeth.

"Gosh, I'm so sorry," Lucky said, scrambling to her feet. "I didn't see you." She offered a hand to the headmistress, pulling her up off the carpet. Then she collected the hair comb, notebook, and pen. "Are you hurt?"

Madame Barrow, headmistress of Barrow's Finishing School for Young Ladies, did not answer the question. Instead, with expertly manicured fingers, she brushed carpet fuzz off her perfectly pressed gray skirt. She set her hair comb back into place, collected the pen and notebook, and then drew a focused breath, filling her lungs as if she were about to dive underwater. Lucky could have sworn that the intake of oxygen added another inch to the headmistress's towering frame. Silence followed. Agonizing silence. Then, after a long exhale, the headmistress spoke. "Do you know how long I have been teaching young ladies of society?" she asked in her thick British accent.

"No, Madame Barrow." Lucky tried not to stare at the headmistress's right eyelid, which had begun to quiver with rage.

"Fifteen years, Miss Prescott. Fifteen *dedicated* years." With a flourish of her hand, she began what Lucky expected would be a long, *dedicated* lecture. "I was raised and educated in England, Miss Prescott, a country that is the pillar of civility and tradition. The patrons of this institution have placed the tender education of their daughters in my capable hands. In my fifteen years here, I have encountered many different sorts of young ladies. But never, and I repeat, *never*, has one child exhibited so much...*spirited energy*."

Spirited energy? Lucky fidgeted. "I know I'm not supposed to run, but—"

The headmistress held up a hand, stopping Lucky mid-excuse. A moment of uncomfortable silence followed. At the other end of the hall, a few students poked their heads out of the tearoom. Eavesdropping. Who could blame them? The scene in the hall was oodles more interesting than the idle chitchat they were forced to engage in while sipping tea. "Must I remind you that running *inside* is not appropriate behavior for a young lady of society?"

"Yes, Madame Barrow. I mean, no, you don't need to

remind me." Lucky shuffled in place. Sarah Nickerson's head appeared next to the others. She smirked. Lucky wanted to holler, "Mind your own business, Sarah!" But she didn't.

"And yet…you ran." The headmistress raised an eyebrow. Lucky scratched behind her ear. She was starting to feel itchy, as if allergic to the headmistress's intense and unblinking gaze.

"I'm sorry?"

"Are you asking me if you're sorry?"

"Um, no, but it's just that…" Lucky's stomach growled. Loudly. "It's just that I didn't want to be late for morning tea."

"Come with me," the headmistress said. As she turned around, Sarah and the other eavesdroppers darted back into the tearoom. Lucky sighed. There'd be no scones today.

The headmistress's office contained lots of lovely things. A collection of china plates graced the walls, lace doilies draped every surface, and a pair of lovebirds twittered in a wicker birdcage.

"How many times have you visited my office this school year?" Madam Barrow asked as she settled into her desk chair.

"I'm not sure." Lucky had lost count.

"Eight times, Miss Prescott. *Eight times.*" Lucky nodded. The incidents streamed through her mind. She'd slid down the entry banister. She'd climbed a ladder to check out a bird's nest on a school windowsill. She'd eaten a cricket on a dare. And there was all the running. "I'm beginning to think that I'm sharing my office with you."

That was a funny thought. Lucky giggled, then tried to take it back but made a snorting sound instead. "Sorry." It was a well-known fact that Madam Barrow did not possess a sense of humor.

The headmistress tapped her fingers on her desk. She seemed more upset than usual, sitting as if a plank were tied to her back. Lucky hadn't been invited to sit, so she stood just inside the doorway, doing her best not to fidget. "This is a finishing school, Miss Prescott. Do you know what that means?"

Of course she did. She'd heard the motto hundreds of times. "Preparing Young Ladies for Society."

"Correct. Young ladies, such as you, enter this school as unformed little lumps of clay. Under my guidance and the tutelage of your teachers, you are shaped—formed—into finished works of art." She smiled, but there was no warmth in the expression.

Lucky didn't like to think of herself as a lump of

clay—or a lump of anything. And she was not quite sure why she had to be turned into a work of art. Works of art were stuck in museums, behind glass or on pedestals. Works of art stayed in one place. That was much worse than being stuck in recitations.

The headmistress opened her desk drawer and took out a piece of writing paper. Then, using her marble pen, she began to write. She paused a moment, glanced up. "You've put me in a difficult position. Are you aware of this?"

"I didn't mean to." Lucky felt a tingle on her ankle, the beginning of a blister. Those shoes were really the worst. Why did every part of her uniform have to be so stiff? She shifted her weight, trying to find relief.

"Are you listening to me?" the headmistress asked.

"Yes." Lucky stopped moving. "I won't run anymore. Really, I won't. I mean, not inside. Unless there's a fire. I have to run if there's a fire. Or an earthquake."

The headmistress sighed. "Miss Prescott, I want all my students to succeed, but I'm beginning to question your chances."

That sounded very serious. Lucky didn't set out to break the rules or to test the headmistress's patience. It just happened. "I know. I'm really sorry. Truly I am. But I saw this cowboy outside and I wanted to…" Leaving school without a parent or guardian was strictly prohibited, and by admitting this, she'd just made things worse.

The headmistress turned red, as if she'd painted rouge over her entire face. "I find I am near my wits' end. How can I be expected to put up with such continued willfulness?"

Willfulness? Lucky wondered. Was it willful to want to see a real, live cowboy up close? Was it willful to want to get somewhere quickly? Was it willful to want a scone? If so, then why was being willful such a bad thing? The problem, in Lucky's opinion, was that there were too many rules and way too much sitting. She couldn't help that her legs got twitchy.

The headmistress began writing again.

"I didn't mean to bump into you. I'm sorry, I really am." Lucky leaned forward. "What are you writing?"

The headmistress wrote a few more lines, then signed her name with a flourish. After folding the paper, she applied a blob of wax and pressed the school's seal into it. "The question you must ask yourself, Fortuna, is *What am I made of?*" She held out the letter. "Please deliver this to your father after school. You are dismissed."

Lucky reluctantly took the letter and was about to head out the door when the headmistress cleared her throat. *Oh, that's right*, Lucky thought. She turned back around and said, "Thank you, Ma'am." The headmistress nodded. Then Lucky made her escape.

On previous occasions, upon leaving the headmistress's office, Lucky had felt a wave of relief. But never before had the headmistress said she was at her wits' end. And never before had she written a letter with a secret message to Lucky's father. There could be nothing good in that letter.

Fortuna Esperanza Navarro Prescott fought the urge to run as she tucked what she believed to be her doom into her pocket.

Calling All Horse Lovers!

Explore the world of DreamWorks Animation's *Spirit Riding Free* with this adventurous new series featuring the innermost thoughts of your favorite PALs!

Share your thoughts using #ReadSpirit